For Nina
D. C.

Also by Davide Cali:
- A Dad Who Measures Up (with Anna Laura Cantone)
- The Bear With The Sword (with Gianluca Foli)
- I Like Chocolate (with Evelyn Daviddi)
- Santa's Suit (with Eric Heliot)
- Piano Piano (with Eric Heliot)
- The Enemy (with Serge Bloch)
- What Is This Thing Called Love? (with Anna Laura Cantone)
- 10 Little Insects (with Vincent Pianina)

First English language edition published in Australia and New Zealand in 2013 by
Wilkins Farago Pty Ltd (ABN 14 081 592 770)
PO Box 78, Albert Park, Victoria, Australia

Teachers Notes and other resources:
www.wilkinsfarago.com.au

© 2012, Editions Sarbacane, Paris

English language translation rights arranged through La Petite Agence, Paris.
English translation © 2013, Wilkins Farago Pty Ltd
Wilkins Farago would like to thank Olivia Snaije for her assistance with the English translation of this book.

National Library of Australia Cataloguing-in-Publication entry

Author:	Cali, Davide.
Title:	The little eskimo / Davide Cali ; illustrator, Maurizio A.C. Quarello .
ISBN:	9780987109958 (hbk)
Target Audience:	For primary school age.
Subjects:	Eskimos--Juvenile fiction.
Other Authors/Contributors:	Quarello, Maurizio A.C.
Dewey Number:	A823.4

Printed by Everbest Printing, China

Davide Cali – Maurizio A.C. Quarello

The Little Eskimo

WILKINSfarago

The Little Eskimo wanted to know two things: he wanted to know if he would be a great hunter when he grew up, and also what was on the other side of the Great Ice Lake…

But the Little Eskimo wasn't allowed to go to the other side of the Great Ice Lake. Everyone knew it was forbidden. He knew would have to wait until he was older to know his future. But how long would he have to wait?

One day, the Little Eskimo met the hare.
'Tell me, Hare, with your big ears, would you happen to
know what's on the other side of the Great Ice Lake?
And have you heard, by chance, if I will become a great hunter?'

'I'm sorry,' said the hare. 'It's true I have big ears, but I
haven't heard anything about this. Ask the fox. He has
a very keen sense of smell. Perhaps he can give you
the answers you are looking for.'

The Little Eskimo went to find the fox.
'Tell me, Fox, with your fine nose, would you happen to have smelled what's on the other side of the Great Ice Lake? And have you smelled, by chance, if I will become a great hunter?'

'I'm sorry,' said the fox. 'It's true I have a keen sense of smell, but I have never smelled anything about this. Ask the owl. She can see everything from up high. It's even said she can see the future. Perhaps she can give you the answers you are looking for.'

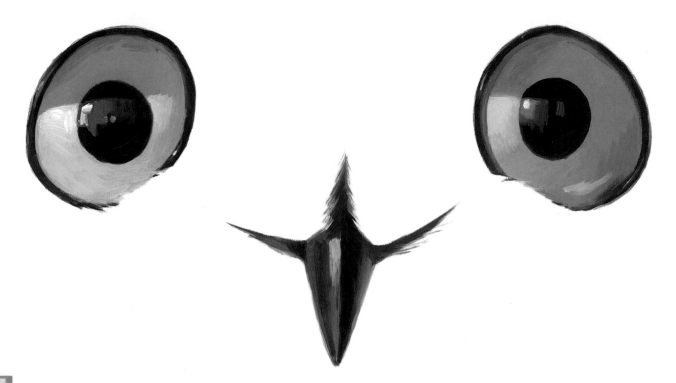

The Little Eskimo went to find the owl.
'Tell me, Owl, you who can see everything from up high, would you happen to know what's on the other side of the Great Ice Lake? And do you know, by chance, if I will become a great hunter?'

'I'm sorry,' said the owl. 'It's true I can see far, far away from high up, but not that far, and I can't see everything. Ask the walrus. He knows about the past. Perhaps he can help you find the answers you are looking for.'

The Little Eskimo went to find the walrus.

'Tell me, Walrus, you who know the past, would you happen to know what is on the other side of the Great Ice Lake? And, by chance, can you tell from the past if I will become a great hunter?'

'I'm sorry,' said the walrus. 'It's true I'm familiar with the past, but I have never traveled to the other side of the Great Ice Lake. All I can say is that I have known many great hunters, and when they were your age, they were just like you. Ask the whale, she knows how to look into our hearts, where everything is written. Perhaps she can give you the answers you are looking for.'

The Little Eskimo went to find the whale. 'Tell me, Whale, you who can look into our hearts, would you happen to know what's on the other side of the Great Ice Lake? And can you see, by chance, if I will become a great hunter?'

'I'm sorry,' said the whale. 'It's true that I can see into people's hearts, and in yours I can tell that you are a courageous little one. But I do not know what is on the other side of the Great Ice Lake, nor if you will become a great hunter. But listen: in the middle of the lake there is a little island. That's where the one who knows all of us lives. It knows you too, without a doubt. Perhaps It can give you the answers you are looking for. If you like, I can take you there.'

So the Little Eskimo, even though he knew that it was forbidden to go to the other side of the Great Ice Lake, climbed onto the whale's nose and together they glided towards the island.

When the whale had dropped him ashore, the Little Eskimo asked:
'What kind of animal should I look for? How will I recognise It?'

'You are on Death's island,' said the whale.
'No-one has ever seen It, no-one knows
what kind of animal It is. But, as I said,
It knows all of us; It will find you.'

The Little Eskimo felt shivers run down his spine. All of a sudden, he understood why no one could go to the other side of the Great Ice Lake. On the other side of the Great Ice Lake was the kingdom of the dead.

'Welcome, Little Eskimo,' said a voice. The Little Eskimo saw a great white moose emerge from the woods.

'Are you Death, who knows us all?'

'Yes, I am.'

'Well, would you happen to know what is on the other side of the Great Ice Lake? And do you know, by chance, if I will become a great hunter?'

Death looked at the Little Eskimo for a moment and then said:

'Come.'

The great white moose led the Little Eskimo to the other side of the island. In the distant fog, the Little Eskimo could see shadows moving.

'There,' said the great white moose.
'That's the other side of the Great Ice
Lake. Do you see the shadows?
Do you know what they are?'

The Little Eskimo thought he knew.
'The shadows of the dead?' he replied.

Death laughed. 'You are wrong, Little Eskimo. They are the shadows of the living.'

'The living?'

'Exactly. What you see is the Land of the Future, and those who will live tomorrow.'

'What does that mean?'

'Until today, you had never ventured to the forbidden side of the lake. If you have arrived this far, it means you are ready for the future. Your future begins today.'

'Does that mean I've grown up?' asked the Little Eskimo.

'Not yet,' replied Death. 'But somewhere over there, there's a Little Eskimo who is a great hunter. There is also a Little Eskimo who is a great fisherman, and even a Little Eskimo who is a great explorer. There are at least ten different Little Eskimos. It is your choice to decide who you will become. It is up to you.'

'How will I know how to find one or another?'
asked the Little Eskimo.

'The shadows of the future do not leave tracks in the snow,'
said Death. 'You are the one who will leave footprints.
You may go where you like and become what you want.'

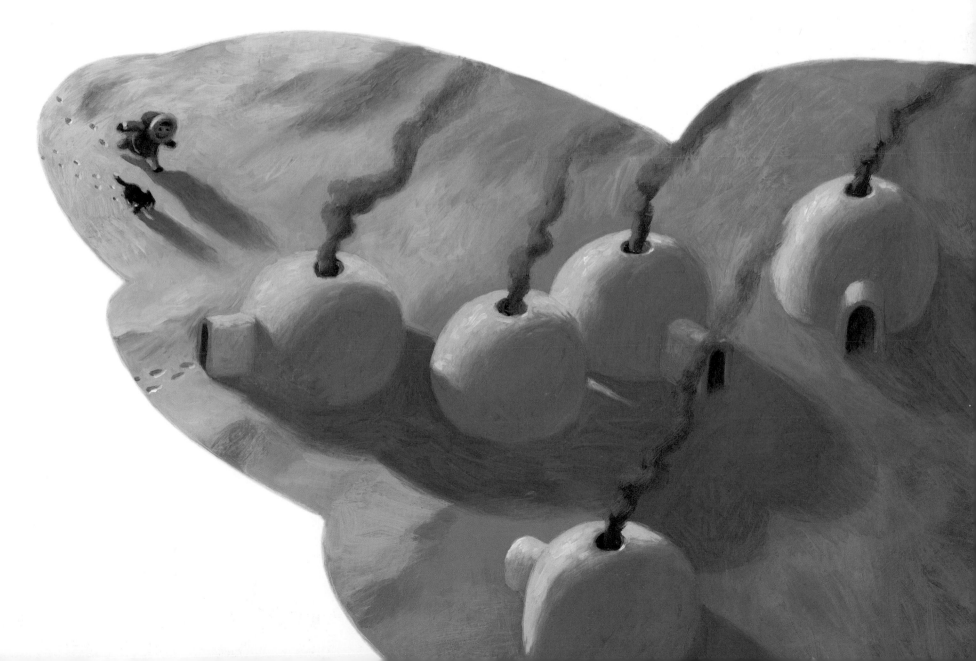

With these words, the great white moose turned and called the whale. Just as the whale surfaced to carry the Little Eskimo back home, the great white moose disappeared into the forest.

That evening, the Little Eskimo went home with an answer and a gift.

He did not know if he would become a great hunter. But he finally knew that across the Great Ice Lake lay the future – or, rather, many different futures.

And he now knew that he could walk towards the future he liked best. That was the gift the great white moose had given him.